THE DENNIS THE MENACE STORYBOOK

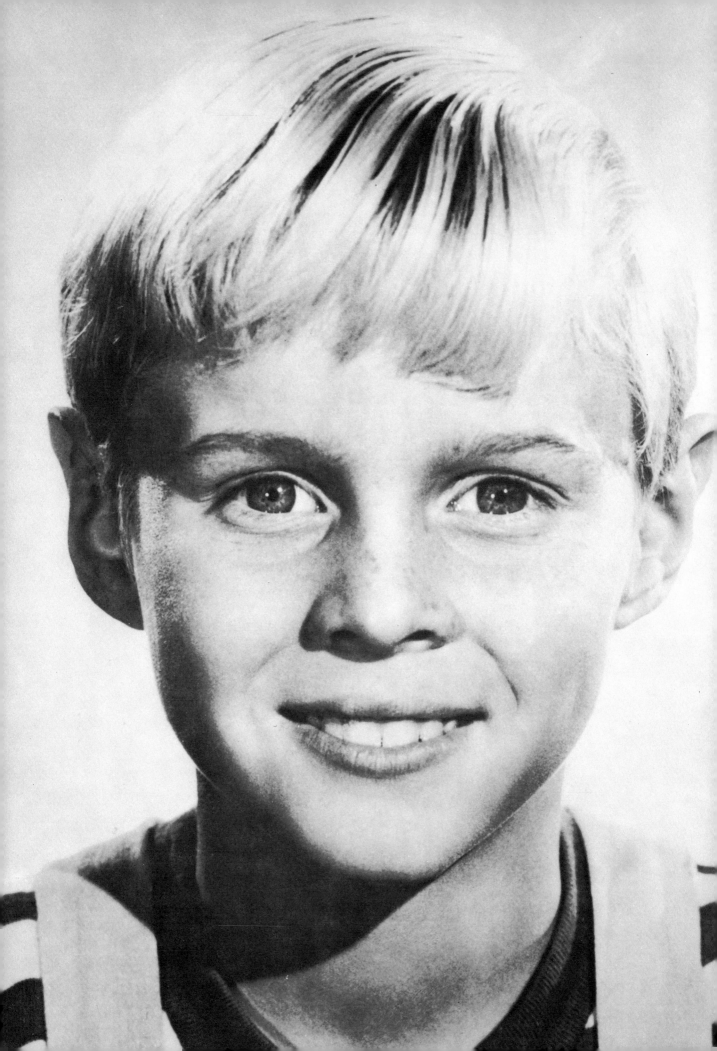

THE DENNIS THE MENACE STORYBOOK

Based on the character created by Hank Ketcham
and adapted by Carl Memling from the television
scripts written by William Cowley,
Peggy Chantler, George Tibbles, and Phil Leslie
Illustrated by Lee Holley

RANDOM HOUSE/NEW YORK

Library of Congress Catalog Card Number: 60-14458

Manufactured in the United States of America

Chapter 1

The Pet Duck

Dennis Mitchell looked at George, and George looked back at Dennis.

Dennis said, "You'd better stop biting people, George."

Then he pressed his nose against the outside of the patio door and peered into the house. No, his mother wasn't in the living room.

Quack, went George, who was a white duck.

"Mr. Wilson was plenty mad when you bit him," Dennis said.

Quack, George replied, waddling about on the patio in quick little darts, as if he didn't have a care in the world.

With a heavy sigh, Dennis picked the duck up and put him in a cardboard carton.

Quack, quack, quack.

Dennis looked hurt. "Shhh," he said. "Mom might hear you, and I've got to sneak you upstairs again!"

Dennis opened the door of the house carefully. Then he started tiptoeing across the living room.

"Is that you, Dennis?" a voice called.

Moving quickly, Dennis hid the carton behind the sofa. Just in time, too! His mother came into the living room carrying a vacuum cleaner.

"Dennis," she said wearily, "your roller skates are still in the middle of the back porch. Now go out and put them away."

Suddenly Dennis's nose started twitching. "Do I smell something burning?" he asked.

"Oh, my goodness!" cried Mrs. Mitchell as she ran toward the kitchen.

At once Dennis raced around the back of the sofa. But before he could pick up the carton, he heard the front door open.

"Hi, son," Mr. Mitchell said. He was carrying a bag of golf clubs.

Dennis straightened up slowly. "Jeepers, Dad," he wailed, "you got back early."

Mr. Mitchell plumped himself down on the sofa and reached for a newspaper.

"Dennis," said Mrs. Mitchell, coming back from the kitchen, "nothing was burning." Then she saw Mr. Mitchell. "Hi, honey."

Dennis stared at the wall behind the sofa. Any moment now George might start quacking again! That would be the end of George. Dennis knew, because he had once asked his father if he liked ducks. Remembering what Mr. Mitchell's answer had been, Dennis shivered.

Now his mother said, "Dennis, I asked you to pick up your skates." And she gave Dennis a look that showed him she meant what she said.

Dragging his feet, Dennis moved slowly toward the porch.

But then Mrs. Mitchell turned on the vacuum cleaner. And the loud hum of the vacuum gave Dennis an idea.

Running back quickly, he said, "Say, Mom, are you going to work that old vacuum when Dad's trying to get some peace and quiet?"

"It's all right, honey," Mr. Mitchell said drowsily from the sofa.

Mrs. Mitchell shook her head. "No, Dennis is right. I wasn't thinking." With these words, she pulled out the plug, and carried the vacuum cleaner and all its parts out of the room.

"Boy," Dennis said sadly, "poor old Mom. I'll bet her back must hurt from carrying all that stuff around."

Mr. Mitchell came wide awake. Looking a little flustered, he sprang up from the sofa and ran to help Mrs. Mitchell.

"Whew!" Dennis sighed with relief. Alone at last!

"Hi, George," he whispered as he picked up the carton. "I bet you thought I forgot all about you."

Quack, went the duck. *Quack, quack, quack.*

Dennis ran upstairs two steps at a time. All the way up to his room he kept pleading, "Shhh, George. My mom and dad might hear you . . ."

Downstairs his parents heard *something*—but not George's quacking. *Thump, thump, thump.* Somebody was pounding angrily on the door of the back porch.

Mr. Mitchell gave a deep sigh. "Come in, Mr. Wilson," he called.

The Mitchells' elderly next-door neighbor came blasting in like a jet. He strode across the porch, and suddenly his feet shot out from under him. As he landed with a thunderous crash, the Mitchells came running out.

"What a place for roller skates!" Mr. Wilson moaned as he was helped to his feet. "Why don't you have Dennis put them away?"

Mr. Mitchell said, "I'm terribly sorry, Mr. Wilson. Is there anything I can do?"

"You can keep that duck out of my yard," Mr. Wilson replied in a choked voice.

Mrs. Mitchell's eyebrows went up. "Duck?" she said.

"What duck?" Mr. Mitchell wanted to know.

"DENNIS'S DUCK!" Mr. Wilson bellowed. "And don't try to tell me that he doesn't have one! Why, that duck even bit me! I was working on my flowers, and he bit me on the back pocket!"

Just then Dennis came out. "Boy," he said, "there's sure a lot of noise here."

"Dennis," Mrs. Mitchell said, "you didn't get around to picking up your skates and Mr. Wilson tripped over them."

"Gee," Dennis said, "I'm sorry."

"Dennis," Mr. Mitchell said, "do you know anything about a duck?"

Dennis looked down at the floor. He shifted uneasily from one foot to the other.

Finally he said, "You mean, do I know that they lay eggs and stuff like that . . .?"

"I mean do you *have* one?" his father persisted.

Dennis hung his head. "I guess so."

"Aha!" Mr. Wilson cried. "Didn't I tell you!"

"Where in the world did you get a duck?" asked Mrs. Mitchell.

"From Charlie Spencer. He moved to New York and he had this swell duck left over from last Easter, so he gave it to me."

"You should have asked permission, Dennis," Mr. Mitchell said.

"I started to," said Dennis. "Don't you remember? You were reading the paper in the living room and I said, 'Dad, do you like ducks?' And you said, 'They're delicious.' "

Mr. Mitchell looked at Mrs. Mitchell. The corners of his mouth twitched.

"We wouldn't eat a pet duck, Dennis," he said.

"I would!" Mr. Wilson said with a snort.

Dennis sighed. "Jeepers, Mr. Wilson, you know what I named him? George. After you. You're my best friend."

"I don't want to be your best friend," Mr. Wilson said. But he wasn't very firm about it.

"Don't you like me, Mr. Wilson?"

Mr. Wilson looked uncomfortable. "Well, sure, Dennis." Gingerly he patted Dennis on the head. "You're a nice boy. You never mean any harm . . . I don't think."

"We'll see that Dennis keeps the duck out of your yard," Mr. Mitchell said.

Turning to leave, Mr. Wilson mumbled, "Thank you."

Those were Mr. Wilson's last words for a while. *Crash!* His feet shot out from under him again.

"Oh-oh," Dennis said. "Dad, you forgot to pick up my roller skates."

Chapter 2

Getting Rid of George

Dennis's father made a pen for the duck in the garage.

First he lined a large carton with straw. Next he filled a big dishpan with water. Then he closed off the duck's corner of the garage with some old chicken wire. And then he went back to the house to finish reading his newspaper.

Dennis stood inside the chicken wire with George. "Well, George," he said, "wasn't this real swell of my dad?"

The duck waddled about, quacking softly and pecking at the cement floor.

"Are you hungry, George?" Dennis asked. "I've got a whole box of slugs and snails over by Mr. Wilson's fence." He pulled back one end of the chicken wire. "So long, George," he called as he ran out of the garage. "I'll be right back with your lunch."

But when Dennis reached Mr. Wilson's fence, he stopped and stared.

Where was George's lunch? The box had tipped over. Jeepers! All the slugs and snails had run away. Poor George!

Dennis hurried back to tell George that lunch would be a little late today. But when he got inside the garage, he stopped and stared again.

WHERE WAS GEORGE?

It took Dennis almost a full minute to see that the wire was open at one end.

"I forgot to close it," he said to himself.

Dennis ran out again and started a frantic search for George.

"Dennis," his mother called, "come in for lunch."

But Dennis kept searching. He had to find George before George could find Mr. Wilson.

"*Dennis Mitchell!*" his father called sternly. "*Come in this instant!*"

Dennis took one last desperate look around. "Please, George, wherever you are," he whispered, "don't upset Mr. Wilson."

A half hour later Mr. Wilson rushed into his own living room. He was carrying a camera and a roll of film.

"Martha," he cried, "there's the most astonishing thing in the back yard. I went out to feed the goldfish and I found a mob of slugs and snails."

Mrs. Wilson didn't look up from her knitting. "What's so astonishing about that?" she wanted to know.

"Martha," said Mr. Wilson, "where is your scientific mind? My dear, when do slugs and snails usually come out?"

Mrs. Wilson was silent for a while. Finally she said, "After dark . . .?"

"Precisely. Well—I have discovered an unknown kind that come out in the hot sun. Furthermore, they travel in herds." By now Mr. Wilson had a faraway look in his eyes. Sighing dreamily, he opened a closet door and said, "I intend to write a scientific paper to read before the garden club. Who knows? This may even win me the presidency of the garden club."

Mrs. Wilson stopped knitting. "Where are you going?" she asked.

"Into the closet," Mr. Wilson said, "to load my camera."

"But why in the closet?" asked Mrs. Wilson.

"I want to make sure the pictures come out. This film is terribly sensitive. The slightest ray of light could ruin it."

As Mr. Wilson marched into the closet, the front doorbell rang. Mrs. Wilson went to answer it.

"Hi, Mrs. Wilson," Dennis said. "Is Mr. Wilson home?"

"Yes, Dennis, come in. He's in the closet."

"He is?" Dennis went over to the closet. "Are you looking for your overcoat in there, Mr. Wilson?" Dennis called.

Mr. Wilson answered in a muffled voice. "No, I'm loading my camera in the dark."

"Oh," Dennis said. But then he frowned. Why was Mr. Wilson loading his camera in the dark? Dennis flipped on the electric switch beside the closet door.

"Is that better now, Mr. Wilson?" he called.

There was a long silence. Then the door opened slowly. The closet was blazing with light, and a roll of spoiled film dangled from Mr. Wilson's hand.

"Martha," Mr. Wilson said wearily, "*please* tell Dennis to go home. . . ."

After Dennis left, Mr. Wilson went back into the closet. This time he loaded the camera without any trouble.

"Now to take those pictures," he said eagerly.

He hurried out to the backyard and went over to the fence. But then he stopped and scratched his head.

"Where can that herd be?" Mr. Wilson wondered. "I'm sure I saw them grazing right around here. . . ."

Then he heard a familiar *quack*. Turning, he saw George swimming in the fishpond. Suddenly George poked his head and long neck under the water and paddled along with his tail stuck straight up.

A stricken look came over Mr. Wilson's face.

"That duck ate all the slugs and snails!" he groaned. "And now he's eating my goldfish!"

"SHOO!" he shouted at George. "SHOO . . .!"

Mr. Wilson was still shouting a few minutes later in the Mitchells' living room. Dennis's father and mother were listening to him with worried looks on their faces.

"That duck has got to go! That duck dug holes in my lawn, he bit me, he ate my goldfish! And now he's robbed me of the presidency of the garden club!" shouted Mr. Wilson.

Dennis gulped. He was sitting on the stairs in the hallway, but he could hear every word.

Dennis's father said, "I'm sorry about all those things, Mr. Wilson."

"Can't we give the duck one more chance?" Mrs. Mitchell pleaded. "Dennis will keep it locked up."

Out in the hallway, Dennis sighed. Good old Mom! No wonder everybody loved mothers!

Thinking of mothers gave Dennis an idea. He jumped up and made a dash for the kitchen.

"Mrs. Mitchell, those goldfish were very valuable," Mr. Wilson said. "There are only a couple left and I don't want to lose them."

Mrs. Mitchell shrugged sadly. "I guess we'll have to get rid of George."

Mr. Mitchell looked very gloomy. "I'll try to explain to Dennis that the duck will be happier at the lake in the park," he said, "and that George will have lots of other ducks to play with there."

"The lake's only three blocks away. Dennis will be able to visit George whenever he wants," Mrs. Mitchell added with a heavy sigh.

They were both so gloomy that they did not see Dennis come into the living room.

"Hi, everybody!" Dennis said.

Mr. Mitchell took a deep breath. "Dennis," he said, "I want to talk to you about the duck."

"You mean George, Dad?" Dennis said. "I think he's going to be a mother. His nest is full of eggs."

"What!" Mr. Mitchell cried.

"Great Scott!" Mr. Wilson said.

Everybody followed Dennis out to the garage.

They found George standing in the pen, preening his feathers. On the straw in George's carton were a dozen shining eggs.

Mr. Wilson frowned. "They look awfully small for duck eggs," he said. He bent down and touched them. "And they're ice cold."

"Dennis," Mr. Mitchell said softly, "you got the eggs out of the refrigerator, didn't you?"

"Yes," Dennis said in a very small voice.

"Well, put them back right away."

"Okay," Dennis said. But as he went to get a box for the eggs, he muttered, "If you give George away, you can just give me away too."

Mr. Wilson whispered, "Mitchell—while Dennis is gone, why don't we grab the duck and jump in my car? We can have him at the lake in three minutes."

Dennis's father looked worried. "I can't do it," he said.

"Of course you can! Put on gloves. Then if he bites, it won't hurt."

"That's not what I mean," Mr. Mitchell went on. "I can't do it because of Dennis. He should at least have a chance to say goodby to George."

Mr. Wilson snorted with disgust. Then, turning on his heel, he said, "I warn you, Mitchell. If you don't get rid of that duck, I will."

With that he marched over to his own house and went straight up to the attic. By the time he came downstairs he was smudged and dirty, but he felt very pleased with himself.

Mrs. Wilson stared at what he was holding in his hand. It was a horn that looked like a thick wooden whistle.

"It's a duck call," Mr. Wilson explained. "I found it in the attic. Hunters use them to lure ducks." Then he added with a chuckle, "In my day I was known as the best caller in the state."

"But what are you going to do with it?"

"I'm going to lure Dennis's duck out of his yard, and then over to the lake in the park."

Mr. Wilson opened a window. Then he raised the duck call to his lips. And then, screwing up his eyes and taking a deep breath, he blew.

Quack, went Mr. Wilson. *Quack, quack, quack.*

Mrs. Wilson looked a little nervous. "If you're going to make that silly noise, please go outside," she said.

"And have Dennis see me?" Mr. Wilson said with a clever smile. "Oh, no. I'll wait till the duck comes into our yard, then I'll go out and lure him down the sidewalk and into the lake."

Mr. Wilson continued honking.

He was still honking when three ducks came sailing in through the open window.

"Great Scott!" Mr. Wilson cried. "They must have heard my call clear over at the park." And he slammed the window shut.

The ducks fluttered about the room, honking excitedly.

"Don't just stand there, George!" Mrs. Wilson screamed. "Catch them and take them outside!"

But Mr. Wilson couldn't move from the window. He stood and stared, his eyes wide with amazement.

Outside, a great flock of ducks filled the air with their honking. They circled above Mr. Wilson's back yard for a while, their feathers glinting in the sunshine. Then, one by one, they dropped down from the sky.

Duck after duck after duck landed on the grass. Soon the back yard was teaming with ducks. And then Mr. Wilson saw Dennis come running out.

"Hi, Mr. Wilson!" Dennis called to him. "George is locked up in the garage—but jeepers, will he be happy when he sees all the friends you got to play with him! Thanks, Mr. Wilson . . . !"

Mr. Wilson staggered back from the window.

"Martha," he groaned, "I must do something about Dennis Mitchell— my nerves have reached the breaking point!"

Chapter 3

The Secret Clubhouse

Every club should have a secret clubhouse. That was what Dennis Mitchell thought. And that was why one Saturday morning Dennis and his friends, Tommy and Stewart, were sitting under his mother's kitchen table.

Dennis was glad his mother used long tablecloths that almost reached the floor. It made sitting under the table feel like being deep inside a shadowy cave.

"I guess this meeting better start," said Dennis.

Then he pounded the floor with a hammer. That was the way meetings always started. Dennis knew because he had once seen a grownup meeting on TV.

"Okay," said Tommy. He was pouring water from an old pitcher into a paper cup held by Stewart.

"Who wants to say something?" asked Dennis.

"Jeepers, I can't think of a thing to say," said Tommy.

Stewart said, "Me neither."

Dennis frowned. "But somebody's got to say something on account of I already banged this hammer."

"I know," Tommy agreed. "Only we can't think of anything to talk about."

"Okay," Dennis said with a sigh. "This here meeting is all over."

Just then they heard the back door being opened. Footsteps came heavily into the kitchen.

"Pull up a chair, Mr. Wilson," they heard Dennis's father say.

There was a scraping noise, then Mr. Wilson answered, "Thank you, Mitchell."

"We're lucky," Dennis's father said. "There's still some hot coffee."

Under the table Dennis listened with dismay. Coffee! Why did grown-ups have to drink so much coffee? When *he* grew up, he would never drink coffee. Only soda! And he would make sure, too, never to drink it on the "roof" of anybody's secret clubhouse.

His father's voice came through the table. "How've you been feeling lately, Mr. Wilson?"

"Great!" answered Mr. Wilson. "Just great!" Then he chuckled. "I *said* I'd do something about Dennis after what happened with those ducks—and I've done it. I've started taking a nerve medicine. And now my nerves are as steady as a rock."

"By golly, that nerve medicine sounds great. Where do you buy it?" asked Dennis's father.

"I don't," said Mr. Wilson. "I make it myself. By the gallon. An old Indian guide gave me the recipe years ago."

Under the table Dennis stiffened. An old Indian guide! Jeepers!

He turned to nudge his friends. But in his excitement, he nudged the water pitcher instead. The pitcher toppled over, and water poured onto Mr. Wilson's foot.

"Great Scott!" cried Mr. Wilson. "Mitchell, your floor is leaking!"

Quickly Dennis's father lifted the tablecloth.

After a moment he found his voice. "Out!" he said. "All of you!"

The three boys crawled out and stood beside the table, shifting uneasily from one foot to the other.

Mr. Mitchell said sternly, "Would you care to explain what's going on here, Dennis?"

Dennis gulped. "Me and Tommy and Stewart were having a club meeting," he said. "And you and Mr. Wilson came in and I accidentally poured water on Mr. Wilson's shoes, and . . ." His voice trailed off weakly. "And I guess that's about all for now."

"Dennis," Mr. Mitchell said gravely, "what do you say to Mr. Wilson?"

"I'm sorry, Mr. Wilson," said Dennis.

"Me, too," said Tommy.

Stewart chimed in. "Me, too. All of us are *awful* sorry Dennis got your foot wet, Mr. Wilson, because now we haven't got a clubhouse."

Dennis's father shook his head. "Under a table is no place for a clubhouse. You need a place that has lots of room and is warm and protected."

Dennis smiled admiringly at him. "Gee, Dad, that's right. You know just about everything, don't you? Where should we look for one?"

"Look around . . . ." his father said wearily. "I'm sure you'll find something."

"Okay, Dad." It made Dennis feel good to hear that his father was so sure they could find a clubhouse. "Come on, guys, let's go out and look around."

Well, that took care of the boys, Mr. Mitchell thought. Now he and Mr. Wilson could sit down again and enjoy their coffee.

They were just finishing a second cup when Mrs. Mitchell and Mrs. Wilson came in. The two ladies had been at a tea, and now they were bubbling with excitement.

"Hi, girls," Mr. Mitchell said with a smile. "Have a good time?"

"I'll say!" exclaimed Mrs. Wilson. "This Madame Tina was at the tea! She's a real, authentic, gypsy fortuneteller." Then, to her husband, "What would you say if I told you that Madame Tina says *you* will hear from Daniel Wilson very soon?"

Mr. Wilson said, "I'd say that was quite a trick." Turning to Mr. Mitchell, he explained, "Daniel Wilson is an ancestor of mine who died during an Indian uprising in 1859."

The two men exchanged amused glances.

Then Mr. Wilson snorted. "I'd like to see any gypsy tell *me* a lot of malarkey like that!" he said.

"Maybe that can be arranged!" his wife said sharply.

Mrs. Mitchell nodded. "Will tomorrow be too soon for you know-it-all gentlemen to meet Madame Tina?" she asked.

Both men were still grinning.

"Then it's all settled," Mrs. Wilson said. "Tomorrow afternoon Madame Tina will be at my house!"

The men's grins stretched all the way across their faces.

Their faces would have sobered very quickly, however, if they had known what Dennis was staring at just then, his eyes shining with excitement.

Tommy and Stewart stood beside him. They too were staring at the trap door on the side of Mr. Wilson's house.

"Boy!" said Dennis. "A secret door!"

Bending, Dennis lifted the trap door. He squeezed through, then stepped down into an open space under Mr. Wilson's house. Tommy and Stewart followed him. The boys peered about in the dimness. All that Tommy and Stewart could see were a few pilings mounted on concrete bases, and some pipes and crossbeams overhead.

But Dennis Mitchell saw much more than that. He let out a joyous yell. "Hey!" *This* can be our clubhouse! And we can't tell anybody because it'll be a *secret* clubhouse," Dennis went on excitedly, "and I'll get a box and we'll make a table out of it and I'll get my dad's hammer . . ."

". . . And *I'll* get a flashlight and some comic books," Tommy said eagerly.

A dreamy look came over Stewart's face. "And I can bring a whole *bunch* of stuff," he said, "because my dad has a real junky garage!"

There followed a very busy day at the Wilson house—both inside the house and under it. Upstairs, Mrs. Wilson was busy all day on the phone making arrangements for Madame Tina's visit the next day. Underground, the boys were busy bringing things to their clubhouse. They made many trips, leaping from bush to bush and tiptoeing across the lawn like Indians.

Dennis brought his father's hammer and a box which, when turned upside down, made a fine table. Then he brought his father's briefcase filled with pencils, papers, and paper cups.

Tommy brought a flashlight and a pile of comic books. He also brought a battered old alarm clock. "It works and everything," he said. "When it goes off it sounds like a real neat rattlesnake."

Stewart brought an old automobile horn with a rubber bulb at the end.

Dennis looked it over carefully. "Boy, this is swell, Stewart!" he said. Then, after a pause, he asked, "What does it do?"

"I don't know," replied Stewart, holding up a pennant that had the words FRANKLIN HIGH on it. "But look at this! It's from my sister's school."

Dennis shook his head with awe. "Say," he said, "that's something! Too bad it's so late now. But I'll bring some nails, and we'll hang your sister's flag up tomorrow."

Chapter 4

The Gypsy Fortuneteller

The next day came—and so did Madame Tina.

The fortuneteller peered into a crystal ball that was on a table in Mrs. Wilson's living room.

"I hear a voice," Madame Tina was saying. "I hear the voice of Daniel Wilson. The voice is small and far away. But he calls . . . he calls . . ."

Mr. Wilson winked at Dennis's father. "Daniel's been calling for quite a while. Maybe I'd better call *him*." And he knocked three times on the table.

There was a long silence, and Mr. Wilson snickered.

But then there came three answering knocks from below.

Thump, thump, thump.

Madame Tina gulped. She was so startled she almost fell off her chair.

Of course, the grownups did not know that there was a secret clubhouse right under them.

The clubhouse was almost all fixed up. Dennis had set up his "table" with papers and pencils. Tommy's battered old alarm clock, tightly wound, was on the "table," too. And so were Stewart's automobile horn and the flashlight. All that had to be done now was to finish hanging up the FRANKLIN HIGH pennant.

Dennis was standing with a hammer on a stack of comic books. The pennant hung slantwise from a cross-beam just over his head.

Dennis held out his hand. "You got another nail, Stewart?" he asked.

Just then Mr. Wilson knocked three more times on the table upstairs.

Thump, thump, thump. Under the house, Dennis pounded the nail into the cross-beam.

This was too much for Madame Tina. Her face turned white and she gave a little scream. "Eeeeek!"

Springing up from her chair, she grabbed her crystal ball. "I . . . uh . . . just remembered, I'm late for another appointment," she stammered. Quickly, she ran out.

Mrs. Wilson and Mrs. Mitchell stared after her, bewildered. But Mr. Wilson laughed so hard that tears streamed down his cheeks. When at last he could catch his breath, he said, "And *that's* the end of Daniel Wilson."

But Mrs. Wilson's eyes were still wide with awe. "George," she said earnestly, "try it again."

So, just to humor his wife and to prove once and for all that she had been fooled by a lot of hocus-pocus, Mr. Wilson tried it again. He knocked three times on the table.

There was a moment's silence.

And then, under the house, Dennis hammered in another nail. *Thump, thump, thump.*

Upstairs there was another moment of silence.

At last Mrs. Wilson said slowly, "Well, George . . . how do you explain *that?*"

Mr. Wilson had no answer. Pushing back his chair, he got up. "Ex-excuse me," he stammered. "I . . . uh . . . think I better go and take some nerve medicine."

Mr. Wilson didn't sleep very well that night. He closed his eyes and lay in the dark, but he couldn't seem to go to sleep. The wind rustling through the leaves of the tree outside his window sounded to him like a small voice calling from far away.

He kept thinking about Madame Tina and about his ancestor, Daniel Wilson. He kept wondering about the strange thumps that had answered

his knocks after Madame Tina had gone. What had made them? Or *who . . .?*

Mr. Wilson tossed and turned.

Then suddenly a thought came to him. He stiffened. Air in the pipe! A pleased smile slowly spread over his face. When air got into a plumbing pipe, it made a loud banging. Of course! That is what it had been! Nothing else!

Now that Mr. Wilson's mind was at ease, he stopped tossing and turning. Soon he was snoring gently, fast asleep.

Along about four o'clock in the morning, however, he was awakened by a strange rattling noise. Mr. Wilson moaned in his sleep. The rattling continued. Mr. Wilson opened his eyes and turned his head to listen.

"Martha!" he called. "Martha!"

"Mmmmm?" Mrs. Wilson murmured sleepily.

"That sound . . . listen."

As suddenly and as mysteriously as it had started, the rattling stopped.

Mr. Wilson thought some more. Then he asked, "Martha, did you set the buzzer on the stove for four in the morning for some reason?"

"Mmmmm—mmmm," murmured Mrs. Wilson. Her eyes were slowly closing. "The buzzer hasn't worked in months."

Mrs. Wilson snuggled down and turned over. "Maybe Daniel is trying to reach you," she said just before dropping off to sleep again.

Mr. Wilson lay down, but his eyes stayed open. And now he kept wondering about the strange rattling. What had made it? Or *who* . . .?

No thought came to ease Mr. Wilson's mind. He tossed and turned and moaned and mumbled the rest of the night.

The next morning Dennis walked along the sidewalk, kicking a stone. "Ouch!" said a man's voice.

Dennis looked up. "Oh, hello, Mr. Wilson."

Mr. Wilson was rubbing his ankle. "Jeepers," said Dennis, "did you get kicked by my rock?" He rushed forward. "Let me rub it, Mr. Wilson. Rubbing's awful good for kicks."

Mr. Wilson backed away nervously. "No, no, thank you, Dennis," he said. "I can do my own rubbing."

Dennis cocked his head to the side and squinted. "What's the matter, Mr. Wilson?" he asked. "Are you sick or something? You look awful."

"*Anybody* who's awakened at four in the morning by a mysterious rattling noise would look awful," Mr. Wilson said bitterly.

"Did you say you heard rattling last night, Mr. Wilson?" asked Dennis.

Mr. Wilson turned on him. "Are *you* still here?" he groaned. "Please, Dennis, go away some place and play. I'm very, very tired this morning."

"Okay," said Dennis. And he went away.

But as he went, he wondered about the rattling noise Mr. Wilson had heard the night before. Stewart's alarm clock made a rattling noise. And Stewart had wound it up very tightly yesterday. Dennis nodded gravely. He'd have to tell Stewart—no more winding.

If that clock kept waking people up at night, people would find out where the secret clubhouse was!

Chapter 5

Who Will Help the Bees?

One day when Dennis was out walking he came to Mr. Swanson's FIXIT SHOP. Mr. Swanson was in the yard putting new screenwire in a door when Dennis arrived.

"Hi, Mr. Swanson," said Dennis. "Need any help?"

"Nope," said Mr. Swanson, who was a man of few words.

"Okay if I watch you, Mr. Swanson?"

"Yep."

Dennis had hardly started watching when he heard a loud buzzing sound.

"Boy," he said, "there sure are a lot of bees around here."

"Yep," said Mr. Swanson. He pointed across the yard.

Dennis turned and saw a row of boxes swarming with buzzing bees. "I know what those are," he said. "Beehives! That's where the bees put their honey." He turned back to Mr. Swanson. "I bet those hives are just full of honey, aren't they, Mr. Swanson?"

"Nope," Mr. Swanson said sadly. Then, taking a deep breath, he went on. "I wish they were. We're not getting honey this year like we should. This late spring's got us all messed up."

Dennis was puzzled. "Late spring?"

"Yep," said Mr. Swanson. "Plants are coming up late this year. There's hardly enough honey around to keep the bees eating."

Dennis frowned. "Gee, if the bees can't find enough to eat, what'll they do?"

Mr. Swanson shrugged gloomily. "Just swarm up and leave, I guess."

"Leave? You mean for good?"

"Yep. And if they do, I may have to go with them. Move to the country some place, I guess."

Dennis looked very serious. "Jeepers, Mr. Swanson, don't move away." Then, lowering his voice, he asked, "Can you keep a secret, Mr. Swanson?"

"Yep."

"I got a club," Dennis whispered. "And we're having a meeting at our secret clubhouse this afternoon. Now don't you worry, Mr. Swanson. I'll make a rule that the whole club should help your bees find honey."

Dennis was the first one at the clubhouse that afternoon. While waiting for the others to come, he cleaned the table. He was shaking the dust off his father's briefcase when Tommy arrived.

Tommy was carrying a clarinet case. "Boy," he said, "taking clarinet lessons is sure dumb." He heaved a sigh. "All that happens is you play for a while and the teacher tells you how terrible it is."

Then Tommy started to sit down. But a sudden loud *honk* made him jump right up again. Tommy was so startled he almost dropped his clarinet case.

Dennis picked up the thing that had honked when Tommy sat down. It was Stewart's automobile horn with the rubber bulb at the end.

"So *that's* what it's for!" cried Dennis.

Delighted, he squeezed the bulb again. *Honk! Honk! Honk!*

Upstairs, Mr. Wilson opened one eye, and then closed it. He was napping on the living-room couch.

Before Dennis could squeeze the bulb again, Stewart came into the clubhouse. He was carrying a toy phonograph.

"Hey, look!" said Tommy. "Stewart's got a hi-fi!"

After Stewart put the phonograph down, Dennis said, "I'll start the meeting now and then you'll make a rule to help Mr. Swanson's bees."

While Tommy and Stewart exchanged puzzled glances, Dennis started the meeting by hitting a water pipe three times with a hammer.

Klang, klang, klang.

Upstairs Mr. Wilson opened both eyes, and looked about dazedly.

"Okay," said Dennis, "this meeting is started."

Stewart's hand shot up. "I want to make a rule before you make your rule about Mr. Swanson," he said. "My rule is that we should listen to the hi-fi first. I got a real neat record with lots of shooting in it."

Then Tommy's hand shot up. "I make the same rule," he said.

"Let me see the record," said Dennis.

Stewart handed it to him, and Dennis stared at the label.

The label said: KIDDIE DISC. TALES OF DANIEL BOONE. BATTLE OF CHEROKEE GAP. PART TWO.

"It's in printing," Dennis said slowly, "and all I can read is writing. But if it's got lots of shooting, I make the same rule, too."

Upstairs, Mr. Wilson was trying to fall asleep again.

Suddenly he sat up with a jerk.

The roar of battle filled the room. Soldiers shouted and rifles cracked.

Mr. Wilson sprang up from the couch.

He gulped. This wasn't air in the plumbing pipes!

This was a battle—with bullets whining through the house and Indians whooping shrilly.

Mr. Wilson stiffened. Indians!

With a heavy sigh, Mr. Wilson flopped back onto the couch.

This time, however, he wasn't napping—Mr. Wilson had fainted.

Down in the clubhouse, the phonograph record spun with a scratchy sound. The Battle of Cherokee Gap was over.

Dennis sighed with pleasure. "That was neat."

Then, remembering about Mr. Swanson, he told his friends about the bee-keeper's trouble. Dennis finished with a rush of words. ". . . And if we don't help his bees find honey, poor Mr. Swanson will have to move away!"

Dennis's friends looked very sad.

"Sure, we'll help," said Tommy.

"Sure . . ." agreed Stewart. "But how?"

Dennis had already given the matter a lot of thought. He said, "Bees get honey from flowers. Right? And *who's* got a whole yard *full* of flowers? With enough honey in them to feed a jillion bees . . .?"

"Who?" asked Tommy.

"Who?" echoed Stewart.

Dennis smiled happily as he gave his answer. "Good old Mr. Wilson!"

The boys ran out to Mr. Wilson's yard and saw that Dennis had been right. There were enough flowers there for a whole barrel full of honey. Row on row of long-stemmed dahlias swayed in the sunlight.

But there were no bees!

The boys stared at one another.

Those big fat dahlias must be just bursting with honey! But why weren't they swarming with buzzing bees?

"Say!" cried Dennis. "I bet I know why. Because they don't have any smell. That's why."

Stepping forward, Tommy sniffed one. "Yeah . . . you're right. They don't smell at all."

"If they smelled good, like honeysuckle and stuff, I bet the bees would go for them," Stewart said sadly.

"Hey!" cried Dennis. "I got it! I KNOW EXACTLY WHAT TO DO! Wait here."

Dennis's plan was very simple. He rushed home and borrowed some perfume from his mother's dressing table. Then back he rushed to Mr. Wilson's yard and sprayed all the dahlias.

"Mmmm. . . ." Tommy sniffed one. "They sure smell good now. Just like my grandpa's apple tree."

"You've got a real smart nose, Tommy," said Dennis admiringly. "Because that's exactly what this perfume is. Apple blossoms."

Stewart said, "Bees like apple blossoms."

"They sure do," Dennis said with a smile. "Can't you hear them?"

Bzzzzzz. Bees came zooming hungrily from all directions, making straight for the scented dahlias. *Bzzzzzz.*

"We better get out of here," said Tommy, "and give them room. We don't want to make them nervous."

"Come on!" yelled Dennis as he started running off. "There's nothing worse than a nervous bee."

Inside the house, Mr. Wilson was feeling very nervous, too.

"Was it a dream?" he asked himself. "Or did I really hear those Indians?" Mr. Wilson stared down at his hands. They were shaking. He started pacing again. He paced straight to where he kept his nerve medicine, and started taking some. He gulped down spoonful after spoonful.

At once he felt calmer.

Mr. Wilson sighed with relief and started humming.

Now he was *sure* it had been a dream . . . !

Mr. Wilson was at peace with the world as he walked out into the yard. He took a deep breath and sniffed the air. Ah-h! The garden smelled good today!

Bzzzzzz! Mr. Wilson ducked and slapped at the air as a bee zoomed by. *Bzzzzzz!* The bee joined all the other hungry bees swarming among the dahlias.

Mr. Wilson stared. Bees feeding on his dahlias? This was strange.

Mr. Wilson was sure he knew all there was to know about dahlias. He had been raising and cross-breeding them for years. And although dahlias were beautiful flowers, he knew that they had no real fragrance. They rarely attracted bees.

Swatting a path for himself through the bees, Mr. Wilson bent over one of the dahlias. He sniffed, frowned, then sniffed again. "Why, they *do* have a fragrance!" he cried excitedly. "A beautiful fragrance! This is sensational!"

"What's sensational?" someone asked.

Mr. Wilson whirled about. "Martha!" he cried. "I've just done it! I don't know how, but I've done it! I crossed just the right dahlias to breed a fragrance into them!"

Mrs. Wilson smiled as she came through the gate. "That's wonderful!" she said.

Wringing his hands with joy, Mr. Wilson said, "What a triumph! I know just the name for them, too. 'The George Wilson Fragrant Dahlias.'" Sighing dreamily, Mr. Wilson went on, "Every gardener in town will be excited. They'll all want one, of course, and I'll have to——"

He paused, his eyes widening. "No! Every gardener in the *country* will be excited about this! Every gardener in the *world!*"

"Oh . . .?" said Mrs. Wilson. "But you haven't got that many dahlias."

"I'll grow them!" cried Mr. Wilson. "I'll have them grown! Acres of them!" He rubbed his hands together and chuckled happily. "Oh, this is going to make horticultural history!"

Mr. Wilson was very busy the rest of the afternoon. He phoned the Merrivale Garden Nursery. And Mr. Merrivale himself came rushing over.

"By golly," said Mr. Merrivale, sniffing at one of the dahlias, "I can't believe it. A scented dahlia! It's sensational!"

"Well, I just *might* let you handle them for me," Mr. Wilson said with a grand air, "*if* you can come up with enough money, that is. If *not,* they go to the highest bidder."

Mr. Merrivale looked hurt. "I hope you're not going to be too hard to deal with now. I've had a bad day."

"Really?"

"That's right. Business is rotten—and to top it off, that neighbor kid of yours was in twice today, pestering me to death!"

"Dennis?" asked Mr. Wilson. "What did he want?"

"Oh, something about flowers and honey and would I leave the hothouse windows open so the bees can get in at night——"

"Well, that's all over and done with," Mr. Wilson interrupted. "Just put your mind on figuring out your best offer for these dahlias."

But before Mr. Merrivale could start figuring, there was another interruption.

"Hi, Mr. Merrivale," called Dennis, climbing over the fence. I saw your truck outside. Were you looking for me?"

"*No!*" Mr. Merrivale said sourly.

Dennis looked hurt. "I thought you came to tell me you changed your mind and that you're going to leave the nursery windows open. The bees won't steal your flowers, Mr. Merrivale. They'll just get the honey out."

Mr. Wilson spoke firmly. "Dennis, go home. Mr. Merrivale and I are talking business."

Dennis tried once more. "Will you leave just *one* window open, Mr. Merrivale?"

Mr. Wilson picked Dennis up and plumped him down on the other side of the fence. "Not another word, Dennis! You're going home right now."

"Can't I come back later to talk over *my* business with Mr. Merrivale?"

"No, Dennis." Mr. Wilson's face was growing red now. "And that's final." Dennis pouted. "Not even *after* later?"

"Sorry." Then, crossing two fingers behind his back, Mr. Wilson said in a gentle voice, "You see, Dennis, Mr. Merrivale and I are going away in a few minutes. Far away. Very far away. A business trip to the North Pole."

"Ohhh," said Dennis, giving up at last. "You'd better not forget to take your gloves, Mr. Wilson," he said sadly. And he walked away, dragging his feet.

When Mr. Wilson joined Mr. Merrivale again, he noticed that the nurseryman's hands were shaking.

"It's that confounded kid," Merrivale muttered. "He's been pestering me all day."

Mr. Wilson nodded wisely. "I know how you feel," he said, "and I have just the thing to steady your nerves."

Quickly Mr. Wilson ran into the house and returned with a bottle of his nerve medicine.

"Say!" cried Mr. Merrivale after drinking a spoonful. "I feel better already. That stuff really works. Where do you buy it?"

Mr. Wilson shook his head. "That medicine can't be bought," he said with a smile. "I make it myself. By the gallon. It's my secret weapon against Dennis Mitchell."

With a flourish, he handed the bottle to Mr. Merrivale. "Here, friend, take it along."

Mr. Merrivale looked very grateful. "Well, thanks," he said pleasantly. "That's just fine." He put the bottle in his pocket and gave a mellow chuckle. Then he started talking business. "Now about those dahlias, George. . . . I'll be honest with you. They're too big for me to handle by myself. But I have a friend, a retired millionaire, who might finance us."

Mr. Wilson had a faraway look in his eyes. "Yes," he said breathlessly. "Go on."

"He's a crotchety old codger," Mr. Merrivale went on, "but he's loaded with money. Now you let me take one of your dahlias and leave it with him tonight—and the three of us will get together tomorrow to talk over the deal."

Just then Mrs. Wilson called from the window: "George, I've just phoned for a cab. Could you carry my suitcase out to the sidewalk? I'm ready to leave for my sister's."

Mr. Wilson turned slowly, like a man in a dream. He had just thought up another name for his great discovery—*Wilsonus fragrantis!*

Mrs. Wilson stared at him. "George," she cried, "is anything wrong? Do you mind my leaving you alone tonight? If you do, just say so."

But all that Mr. Wilson could say as he walked dreamily toward the window was, "Sensational . . . it's sensational. . . ." over and over again.

Chapter 6

The House <u>Is</u> Haunted!

"Can Tommy stay for dinner and then sleep here the whole night?" Dennis asked.

Mrs. Mitchell brushed Dennis's hair back from his forehead. "Why, of course, Dennis. But shouldn't he ask his mother first?"

"I don't have to," Tommy said with a grin. "She already said yes."

So Tommy stayed for dinner, and it was delicious. But as for sleeping the whole night—that didn't work out too well.

Things started going wrong the moment Mr. Mitchell found out that Dennis had borrowed his briefcase.

"Dennis, I've warned you before about taking other people's things without asking!" Mr. Mitchell said sternly. "Now, where's my briefcase?"

"In our clubhouse," Dennis mumbled.

Mr. Mitchell said, "I want you to go to your clubhouse, wherever it is, and get it!"

"Does it have to be right now, dear?" asked Mrs. Mitchell. "The boys should be in bed."

"Well . . . all right," Mr. Mitchell said grudgingly. But then he gave Dennis a long, hard look. "That briefcase is very important to me, Dennis. I want it in this house first thing in the morning!"

Dennis hung his head. "Gee, I'm real sorry, Dad."

As the boys went upstairs, Tommy whispered, "Golly, Dennis, your dad sure is mad at you."

"Yeah. . . ." Dennis said miserably. "I know."

They undressed slowly and put out the lights. They got into bed and soon Tommy was asleep. Dennis lay beside him with his eyes wide open.

The night grew darker and darker. The hours passed slowly.

Suddenly Tommy mumbled something and thrashed out with his feet.

"Hey," Dennis said, "quit kicking!"

Tommy sat up, rubbing his eyes. "Didn't you *never* go to sleep?" he asked Dennis.

Dennis shook his head gloomily. "Nope. I want to stay awake all night so I can get my dad's briefcase first thing in the morning."

Tommy sighed. "Yeah…" he said. "Your dad sure was mad at you."

A thought struck Dennis. "Hey, Tommy," he said, "you want to get it right now?"

"Won't your folks wake up?" yawned Tommy.

"Nope. Because I got a secret way to get out."

Tommy flung the blanket off and both boys jumped out of bed. As they put their robes on, Dennis said, "My dad's sure going to be glad when he wakes up and there's his briefcase."

Then Dennis got a flashlight and they both left by the secret way—out through Dennis's bedroom window and down the drainpipe to the ground.

They tiptoed across the dark, slippery grass and crouched by the trap door.

Dennis clicked the flashlight on.

"Shhh," Tommy whispered. "Don't make any noise."

"It's okay," said Dennis in his normal voice. "Nobody's home. Mrs. Wilson is at her sister's—my mom told me. And Mr. Wilson went on a faraway business trip all the way to the North Pole. He told me so himself."

They went through the trap door and Dennis's flashlight probed the darkness under Mr. Wilson's house.

"Hey, look," said Dennis, pointing up at a cross beam. One side of the FRANKLIN HIGH pennant had torn loose. It hung limp and bedraggled.

Dennis frowned. "We better fix it," he said.

Upstairs, Mr. Wilson was smiling, murmuring happily in his sleep. He hadn't slept this well ever since Dennis Mitchell first moved next door. Nor had he ever dreamed as pleasant a dream as the one he was having now.

"*Wilsonus fragrantis . . .*" Mr. Mitchell murmured happily. "'The George Wilson Fragrant Dahlia'. . . ."

Thump, thump, thump.

Mr. Wilson stopped murmuring. The smile faded slowly from his face. He stirred uneasily in his sleep.

Thump, thump, thump.

Mr. Wilson's eyes opened. They popped. They rolled nervously, staring at the darkness.

Under the house, the pennant was hanging straight again, and Dennis had found his father's briefcase. The boys were moving toward the trap door when Tommy stumbled over his clarinet.

Tommy stared at it with distate. "I must've left it here before," he said. Then he added sadly, "I better take it home."

But Dennis had another idea. "Let's hear you play it," he said.

"Okay," said Tommy.

As Dennis moved around looking for a place to sit, he stepped on the automobile horn.

Honk.

Upstairs, Mr. Wilson clutched at his chest and groaned.

Raising the clarinet to his lips, Tommy started to blow. A weird wailing filled the clubhouse.

Dennis winced. No wonder Tommy's music teacher told him his playing was terrible! It sounded worse than the howling of a dog and the meowing of a cat and the shriek of a skidding tire all mixed together.

It sounded so terrible that Mr. Wilson jumped out of bed and ran out into the street in his pajamas yelling, "Help! The house *is* haunted! Help!"

Chapter 7

Thank You, Dennis!

Lights clicked on and window shades flew up all along the street.

Mr. Wilson was staggering about, sobbing and clapping his hands to his head when Dennis's father came rushing over.

It took almost twenty minutes, almost a whole bottle of nerve medicine, and almost a whole percolator of strong black coffee before Mr. Wilson was himself again.

But he came close to breaking down again when Mrs. Mitchell marched into the kitchen herding Dennis and Tommy before her.

"Guess where I found these two boys just now," she said. "They were climbing in through Dennis's bedroom window."

And then the whole story came out. About the secret clubhouse. About the thumping, the rattling, the honking, and the sounds of battle.

Mr. Wilson groaned as he listened. But he was really pleased to learn that his ancestor, Daniel, had never really tried to contact him.

And Mr. Mitchell listened with a stern look, but it pleased him to hear that Dennis had been so anxious to fetch his briefcase for him.

By now dawn had begun to streak the sky, and with the lightening of the sky Mr. Wilson's mood lightened, too. He started thinking of his amazing dahlias again.

"Have I told you about my amazing discovery?" he asked Mr. Mitchell. And then he told all about it.

"This whole thing is fascinating," Mr. Mitchell said. "I never thought about it before, but dahlias don't have any particular odor, do they?"

Mr. Wilson beamed. "Not till my discovery, they didn't." Then he got up. "If you have a minute to spare, come over and let me show them to you," he said.

So all the grownups marched out to sniff the dahlias. And that was when they came upon Dennis spraying.

They all stood, frozen, shocked. Tears formed in Mr. Wilson's eyes, and his mouth opened and closed, like a fish out of water. Finally he forced some words out. "You—you—Dennis! You mean the fragrance—it—was—all—you. . . ."

"Yep," Dennis said proudly. "The bees like it. And now Mr. Swanson won't have to move away. All because I made your dahlias smell so sweet."

Mr. Wilson moaned. He was about to sag to the ground when Mr. Merrivale and a tall, well-dressed man walked briskly up the garden path. The man grasped Mr. Wilson's hand, saving him from falling, and pumped it hard.

"Mr. Wilson," he said, "I'm Mark Stacy. I won't waste time. I think we've got a great thing here, and you and I can do some business with it."

Mr. Wilson whimpered.

"Yes, sir," Mr. Stacy continued. "I want to talk to you about this wonderful nerve medicine of yours!"

Mr. Wilson's jaw dropped.

Mr. Stacy went on: "Mr. Merrivale here gave me some of the stuff when he dropped by last night and my nerves haven't been this calm in twenty years! If you'll sell me the formula on a royalty basis—we're in business, Mr. Wilson!"

This was when a look of slowly spreading delight started shining in Mr. Wilson's face.

And this was when Mr. Wilson turned around and said: "If it wasn't for you and the bees, I never would have met Mr. Stacy. . . . In fact, if it wasn't for you, I would never have made the nerve medicine. THANK YOU, DENNIS!"